Dear Parents and Educators,

Welcome to Penguin Young Readers! As parent[s], [you]
know that each child develops at his or her own [rate in]
speech, critical thinking, and, of course, reading. Penguin Young
Readers recognizes this fact. As a result, each Penguin Young Readers
book is assigned a traditional easy-to-read level (1–4) as well as a
Guided Reading Level (A–P). Both of these systems will help you choose
the right book for your child. Please refer to the back of each book
for specific leveling information. Penguin Young Readers features
esteemed authors and illustrators, stories about favorite characters,
fascinating nonfiction, and more!

Three up a Tree

LEVEL **3**

GUIDED
READING
LEVEL **J**

This book is perfect for a **Transitional Reader** who:
- can read multisyllable and compound words;
- can read words with prefixes and suffixes;
- is able to identify story elements (beginning, middle, end, plot, setting, characters, problem, solution); and
- can understand different points of view.

Here are some **activities** you can do during and after reading this book:
- Story Map: A *story map* is a visual organizer that helps explain what happens in a story. On a separate sheet of paper, create a story map for one of the stories in this book. The map should include the setting (where and when the story takes place), characters (who is in the story), problem (the difficulty in this story), goal (what the characters want to happen), events (list three things that happen in the story that help the characters reach their goal), and ending (how the characters solve the problem and reach their goal).
- Creative Writing: In this story, Lolly, Spider, and Sam take turns telling stories that include some of the same characters. Pretend it is your turn to tell a story starring some of the same characters (the chicken, for example).

Remember, sharing the love of reading with a child is the best gift you can give!

—Bonnie Bader, EdM
  Penguin Young Readers program

*Penguin Young Readers are leveled by independent reviewers applying the standards developed by Irene Fountas and Gay Su Pinnell in *Matching Books to Readers: Using Leveled Books in Guided Reading*, Heinemann, 1999.

For Toby Sherry—JM

Penguin Young Readers
Published by the Penguin Group
Penguin Group (USA) Inc., 375 Hudson Street, New York, New York 10014, USA
Penguin Group (Canada), 90 Eglinton Avenue East, Suite 700, Toronto, Ontario M4P 2Y3, Canada
(a division of Pearson Penguin Canada Inc.)
Penguin Books Ltd, 80 Strand, London WC2R 0RL, England
Penguin Ireland, 25 St Stephen's Green, Dublin 2, Ireland (a division of Penguin Books Ltd)
Penguin Group (Australia), 707 Collins Street, Melbourne, Victoria 3008, Australia
(a division of Pearson Australia Group Pty Ltd)
Penguin Books India Pvt Ltd, 11 Community Centre, Panchsheel Park, New Delhi—110 017, India
Penguin Group (NZ), 67 Apollo Drive, Rosedale, Auckland 0632, New Zealand
(a division of Pearson New Zealand Ltd)
Penguin Books (South Africa), Rosebank Office Park, 181 Jan Smuts Avenue,
Parktown North 2193, South Africa
Penguin China, B7 Jiaming Center, 27 East Third Ring Road North,
Chaoyang District, Beijing 100020, China

Penguin Books Ltd, Registered Offices: 80 Strand, London WC2R 0RL, England

Text and illustrations copyright © 1986 by James Marshall. All rights reserved. First published in 1986 and 1989 by Dial Books for Young Readers, an imprint of Penguin Group (USA) Inc. Published in a Puffin Easy-to-Read edition in 1994. Published in 2013 by Penguin Young Readers, an imprint of Penguin Group (USA) Inc., 345 Hudson Street, New York, New York 10014. Manufactured in China.

The Library of Congress has cataloged the Dial edition
under the following Control Number: 86002163

ISBN 978-0-14-037003-4   10 9 8 7 6

PENGUIN YOUNG READERS

LEVEL
TRANSITIONAL
READER
3

THREE
UP A TREE

by James Marshall

Penguin Young Readers
An Imprint of Penguin Group (USA) Inc.

The Tree House

"Wow!" said Spider.

"Will you look at *that*!"

Some big kids down the street

had built a swell tree house.

"Can we come up?" called out Sam.

"No!" said the big kids.

"Well!" said Spider.

"Never mind," said Sam.

"We'll build our own tree house."

"Let's ask Lolly to help,"

said Spider.

But Lolly would not help.

"I'm too busy," she said.

"You call *that* busy?" said Spider.

"Let's go," said Sam.

In no time Spider and Sam

were as busy as squirrels.

Meanwhile Lolly decided

to take a little snooze.

When Lolly woke up

the tree house was finished.

"Wow," she said.

"I'll be right up."

"Oh no," said Sam.

"You didn't help."

"Oh *please*," said Lolly.

"No!" said Spider.

"I know some good stories,"

said Lolly.

"Stories?" said Sam.

"I love a good story."

Lolly was up the tree in a flash.

"Now tell us a story," said Sam.

"And make it good," said Spider.

"Sit down," said Lolly.

"And listen to this."

Lolly's Story

One summer evening
a doll and a chicken
went for a walk.
And they got lost.
"Oh no," said the doll.

Just then a monster

came around the corner.

"Oh no," said the doll.

"Let's run!"

cried the chicken.

And they ran as fast

as they could.

"He's right behind us!"

cried the chicken.

"Oh no!"

said the doll.

"Quick!" cried the chicken.
"Let's climb that tree!"
And they did—
in a jiffy.
But monsters know how
to climb trees, too.

"He's got us now!" cried the chicken.

"Oh no!" cried the doll.

The monster opened his mouth.

"Will you tie my new shoes?"

he said.

"Oh yes!" said the doll.

"Not much of a story,"

said Spider.

"The end was too sweet."

"Can you tell a better story?"

said Lolly.

"Listen to this," said Spider.

Spider's Story

A chicken caught the wrong bus.

She found herself

in a bad part of town—

the part where the foxes live.

"Uh-oh," she said.

Quickly she pulled down her hat
and waited for the next bus.
But very soon—you guessed it—
a hungry fox came along
and sat beside her.

His eyes were not good.

But there was nothing wrong

with his nose.

"I can smell that you're having

chicken tonight," he said.

"Er . . ." said the chicken.

"Yes, I have just been to the store."

"I *love* chicken,"

said the fox.

"How will you cook it?"

The chicken knew

she had to be clever.

She did not want the fox

to invite himself to dinner.

"Well," she said.

"I always cook my chicken

in sour chocolate milk

with lots of pickles and rotten eggs."

"It sounds delicious,"

said the fox.

"May I come to dinner?"

"Let's see," said the chicken.

"That will make ten of us."

Well, *that* was too many

for the fox!

He grabbed the chicken's grocery

bag and ran away.

"All for me!" he cried.

"All for me!"

The poor chicken flew up
into a nearby tree
to wait for the next bus.
(She should have done that
in the first place.)

P.S. When the fox got home,

he reached into the bag.

But there was no chicken inside.

Only the chicken's favorite food.

Can you guess what it was?

"Worms!" cried Lolly.

"Worms!

That story wasn't bad."

"Not bad at all," said Sam.

"But now it's *my* turn."

Sam's Story

A monster woke up from a nap.

He was *very* hungry.

"I want ice cream," he said.

"Lots of it."

He went out to buy some.

But he got lost.

"Oh well," he said.

"I'll just ask someone for help."

At that moment a fox

came around the corner.

"Excuse me," said the monster.

"Help!" cried the fox.

"I'm getting out of here!"

And away he went.

"How rude," said the monster.

He put on the fox's hat,

scarf, and glasses.

Just then a doll and a chicken

came around the corner.

"Hi," said the chicken.

"Will you help me find

some ice cream?" said the monster.

"If you will give us a ride

in your wagon," said the chicken.

And off they went.

"Stop!" said the chicken.

"This is the place for ice cream."

"Oh really?" said the monster.

"Wait here," said the doll.

"We'll be right back."

In a moment they were back.

"Step on it!" said the doll.

"You don't want your ice cream

to melt!"

"I'll hurry!" said the monster.

"Faster!" cried the chicken.

The monster ran as fast as he could.

Soon they came to a big tree.

"This is where we live,"

said the doll.

And they all climbed up the tree.

The doll and the chicken

opened their bags.

But there was

no ice cream inside.

There was only money.

"Oh no!" said the monster.

"You are bank robbers!"

The monster took off his hat,

scarf, and glasses.

The doll and the chicken

were scared out of their wits.

"Help, help!" they cried.

"Let's get out of here!"

And they ran as fast as their

little legs could carry them.

The monster returned

the money to the bank.

As a reward he was given

all the ice cream he could eat.

And there was *lots* of it!

"My story was better," said Lolly.

"No, mine was," said Spider.

"No, mine!" said Sam.

"Let's hear them again," said Lolly.

And they did.